SNIP SNAP, ALLIGATOR!

Written by Mara Bergman ✳ Illustrated by Nick Maland

KU-637-394

Hodder
Children's
Books

A division of Hachette Children's Books

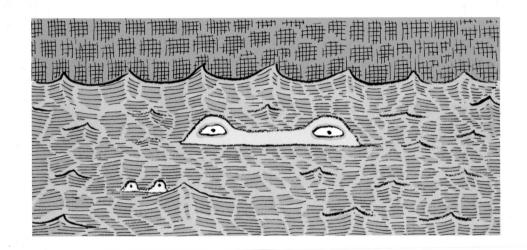

This snappy book belongs to:

....

WITHDRAWN

9030 00003 3154 1

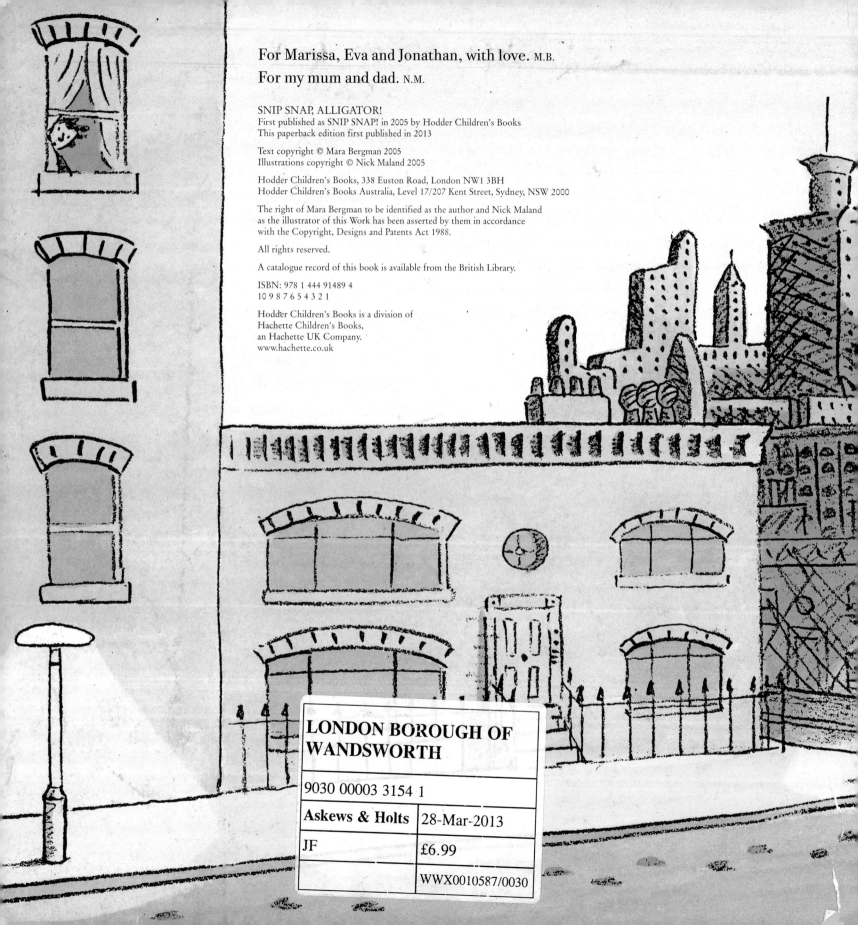

For Marissa, Eva and Jonathan, with love. M.B.

For my mum and dad. N.M.

SNIP SNAP, ALLIGATOR!
First published as SNIP SNAP! in 2005 by Hodder Children's Books
This paperback edition first published in 2013

Text copyright © Mara Bergman 2005
Illustrations copyright © Nick Maland 2005

Hodder Children's Books, 338 Euston Road, London NW1 3BH
Hodder Children's Books Australia, Level 17/207 Kent Street, Sydney, NSW 2000

The right of Mara Bergman to be identified as the author and Nick Maland
as the illustrator of this Work has been asserted by them in accordance
with the Copyright, Designs and Patents Act 1988.

All rights reserved.

A catalogue record of this book is available from the British Library.

ISBN: 978 1 444 91489 4
10 9 8 7 6 5 4 3 2 1

Hodder Children's Books is a division of
Hachette Children's Books,
an Hachette UK Company.
www.hachette.co.uk

LONDON BOROUGH OF WANDSWORTH	
9030 00003 3154 1	
Askews & Holts	28-Mar-2013
JF	£6.99
	WWX0010587/0030

When the alligator
came *creeping...*
creeping...

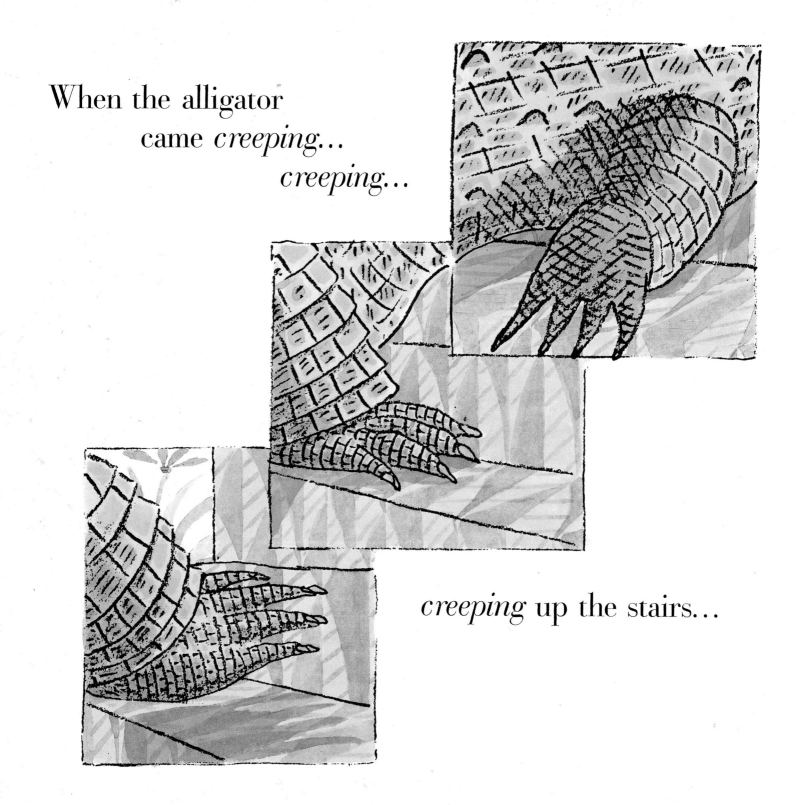

creeping up the stairs...

...were the children scared?

YOU BET THEY WERE!

Marissa tried to close the door.
Eva tried and tried some more.
And Jonathan didn't try at all,
he just cried and cried and cried...

...then he hid.

The alligator's mouth was wide.
Its teeth were long.
Its jaws were strong.
The children watched as it began
to bite the edges of the door.

SNIP SNAP
SNIP SNAP
snip snap
snap snip !

Were the children scared?

YOU BET
THEY WERE!

The alligator
slithered...
slithered...
slithered
down the hall –

and slipped into the sitting room.

It *swishhhhhhed* and *swoooooshed* its tremendous tail, which was shiny and spiked and full of scales.

Were the children scared?

YOU BET THEY WERE!

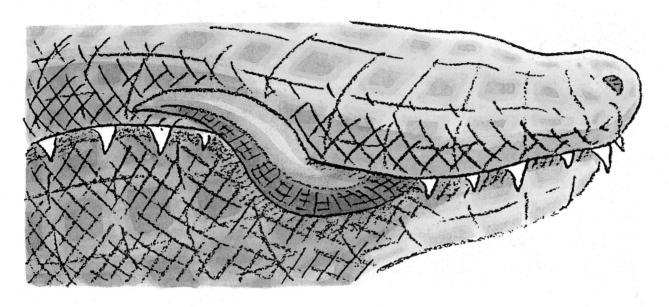

The alligator's tongue was flicking.

The alligator's feet were kicking.

Then the alligator's mouth
opened up v-e-r-y wide
creak...creak...creak...

as if to invite the children inside.

Were the children scared?

YOU BET THEY WERE!

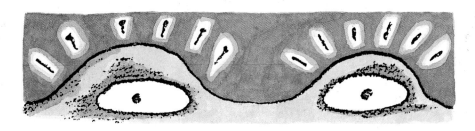

The alligator's eyes were flashing.

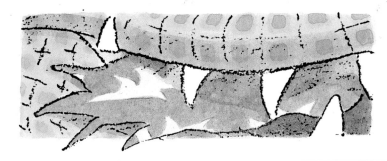

The alligator's teeth were gnashing
as tables and chairs and piano went crashing.

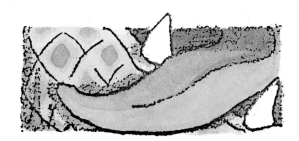

And after the sofa and curtains were ripped
the alligator licked its lips.

Were the children scared?

YOU BET THEY WERE!

And then what did the alligator do?
Did it say to the children,
'I'm going to eat you?'

Well, not exactly, but…

it came closer…

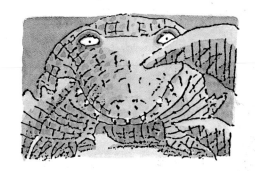

and closer…

and closer until…

The children decided they'd had enough
of all this scary alligator stuff.
They plucked up their courage
and gave a great shout:

'ALLIG
YOU
GET C

ATOR,

UT!'

And was the alligator scared?

YOU BET IT WAS!

Thump bump

bump

thump!

...all the way home!